HEY YOU!

Why the heck would I take time out of my galaxy-saving schedule to write a survival guide? Because I feel like it, that's why! And hopefully, by the time I've given you enough sensitive information to get you arrested by the Nova Corps, you'll be ready to give us a hand. Nobody can do it alone. Not even me, and I'm the toughest thing going.

There's another reason. Our ship, the <u>Milano</u>, is busted and I'm on this planet called Berhert. Who names a planet Berhert? Maybe a guy named Berhert? But, then I wonder: Who names a kid Berhert? Answer me that!

Yeah, the Guardians and I are taking a bit of a break from one another. Don't worry! It's temporary—at least <u>I think they're coming back</u>. I get the feeling they're not so crazy about me sometimes. They're like, "Rocket, stay here and repair the ship," and, "Rocket, don't let Nebula escape because she might try and kill you." Like a moron, here I am.

That's why I need you to pay attention. Because one day, you're gonna be a hero, too. Maybe then, we can team up. But don't get any big ideas—you ain't a hero, yet. I mean, you haven't even turned the page, right?

GROOT AND ME A WHILE BACK... HE WOULD FIT INSIDE MY POCKET NOW!

Ah, the good old days. This is from when I was solo—except for Groot, of course—and did whatever the heck I wanted. I wonder whether things were better then. Like right now, I have to repair a starship on a planet that's almost entirely covered in trees. Guess what covers the rest of it? Mud! Try getting spare parts in a place like this—those trees ain't selling!

Back to my picture. Notice how they went out of their way to make me look short? Could have just tilted the camera down, but no—that'd be showing too much respect. This is what I'm talking about, kids: if you want to be taken seriously, get a bigger crew, like I did.

TAKE THAT,
WANTED POSTER
PHOTOGRAPHER!

GUARDIANS

Before I thrill you with the story of our Abilisk battle, I'm gonna throw another rule at you. Think sharp, they're coming fast.

RULE #2

BE PROFESSIONAL

This is something I try for and, I admit, maybe don't always succeed at doing. Gimme a break! <u>You try working with this crew—</u> the Guardians are about as orderly as the Collector's basement.

To make this crystal clear, a reminder on how we all met. Groot and I, doing our bounty hunter bit, came to Xandar—a planet of idiots—hoping one of the Xandarians had a price on his or her empty head.

Recently, I've been rolling with the Guardians—doing good, and taking a little for ourselves while we've been at it. Nothing wrong with that, right?

We've been on a job for the Sovereign, a bunch of stuck-up Goody Two-shoes with zero sense of humor. They had another problem, too: This monster, an Abilisk, was wrecking their power station. I'm not sure how it did this exactly. Maybe it slobbered everywhere.

When we showed up, Quill used this goofy tracker to find the Abilisk, but I think all he really wanted was to get a rise out of Gamora. And I, nice guy that I am, wired up a stereo so Quill could have some music. Trust me, he fights better with it. Plus, it drowns out Drax's grunting, which can get distracting.

But suddenly, Quill was saying that he didn't want a stereo, and the others thought I should be doing something more useful. What do they know? Do I tell them what to do? The Guardians. Sometimes it's love, but often it's tolerance. Why? See Rocket's Rule #1.

RULE #1 | PEOPLE MAKE NO SENSE.

Our debate—argument, really—was cut short, because the Abilisk showed up. And the Sovereign weren't exaggerating: This was a real-deal monster.

I WOULDN'T MESS WITH THIS GUY.

APPROACH

ARMED AND

BACK VIEW

SIDE VIEW

PRISONER 45-GY

USE EXTREME
CAUTION

COULD SWEAR THERE WAS
ONE AT IOOK. I DARE YA TO
CALL ME A LIAR!

REWARD: 20,000 UNITS

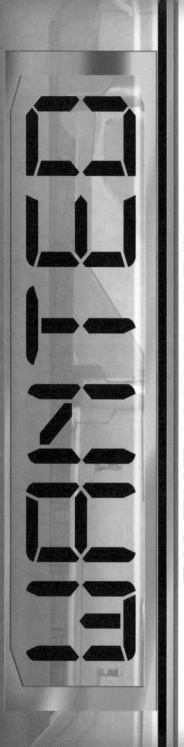

Groot was drinking from a public fountain—and <u>not a drinking fountain</u>—while I scanned one irritating Xandarian after another.

I saw Quill, and then I saw his bounty: forty thousand. With that, we could buy a ship, blow it up just for fun, and then buy another one. But we weren't the only guests at this party. Gamora was there, too. And that's when the chaos started.

Pretty soon, Groot was grabbing the wrong person, Gamora was biting me (so mature!), and Quill kept getting away. That is, until—galaxy-size misfortune—the Nova Corps arrested all of us. I hate complicated jobs. And this one had barely just begun.

The Nova Corps shipped us off to the Kyln. Imagine the place you most want to go on vacation, and then picture its opposite. Did you think of a floating prison stuck in an asteroid field at the edge of space? That's the Kyln.

I was gonna bust out with Groot and Quill—remember that fat bounty? This meant we had to keep the other prisoners from turning Quill into puddle of goo. He didn't make that easy. Bounty hunting can be uncomplicated—that is, unless your bounty starts annoying psychos with names like Drax the Destroyer.

Because when Drax went after Gamora, Quill tried to save her. Not that she needed much help. Soon enough, all of us—including Drax—were teaming up to escape that stinking cage. Was this my first plan? No. Did I roll with it? Yes, because:

YOU NEED TO BE FLEXIBLE.

Being flexible ain't easy, believe me, but it's the only way I've managed to stick with these jokers.

And on the Kyln, it worked—we got out, and everyone had me to thank for it. Not that anyone actually did thank me, of course. Doesn't really matter, because we were on our way to becoming the greatest superteam in the galaxy.

Seriously, is there a better crew, <u>anywhere?</u>

RULE #4

IF YOU HAVE TO FIGHT, FIGHT SMART.

Don't even look at a picture of an Abilisk—the thing is like your least favorite internal organ that sprouted giant tentacles and grew a huge mouth, which it totally forgot to floss or brush. But just in case you ever need to take one down, here are some good old-fashioned dos and don'ts:

DON'T waste ammo on the Abilisk's hide. That skin is like blast shielding.

That tough outside might tempt you to think the inside is softer than a mattress made of kittens. But before you try anything:

DON'T jump into the Abilisk's mouth, believing you can attack it from inside.

Drax did this, hacking and slashing like the Abilisk ate a can of soup, including the can opener. This beast is two-way tough. Except, as Quill noticed, one tiny soft spot near the neck. So:

DO make the Abilisk raise its head, exposing its weak point.

Quill and I acted as decoys—and were within inches from getting crushed—while Gamora made a crazy did-you-see-that jump, hit the weak spot, and cut the Abilisk wide open.

Drax fell right out, <u>thinking he'd killed it</u>. I was going to break the news to him, but I was too busy escaping the smell. Seriously, Abilisks must eat space garbage.

So if you face an Abilisk, that's what you do. No pressure.

I bet you're wondering why Groot didn't rip that Abilisk in half. Ordinarily no problem, but right now Groot would fit in your hat. Not that he would like that—he hates hats. Actually, it's worth doing that properly:

RULE #5

GROOT HATES HATS.

You definitely want to be on Groot's good side, even when he's small, like he is now.

Groot's been like this ever since the Battle of Xandar, and his new situation has turned me and the others—all right, mainly me—into sorta parents. Besides, who else is gonna look after the little guy?

It's weird. Suddenly I'm worried about what he eats, because otherwise he might chomp on a bug that's been living in an Abilisk's armpit.

Some days are good . . . other days we do laundry.

I care about Groot—always will—but feeling responsible for someone else is strange. I'm hoping he'll grow up soon, so he can watch my back instead of the other way around. But I won't rush him. After what he did on the Dark Aster, we owe him. I mean, he did save us all.

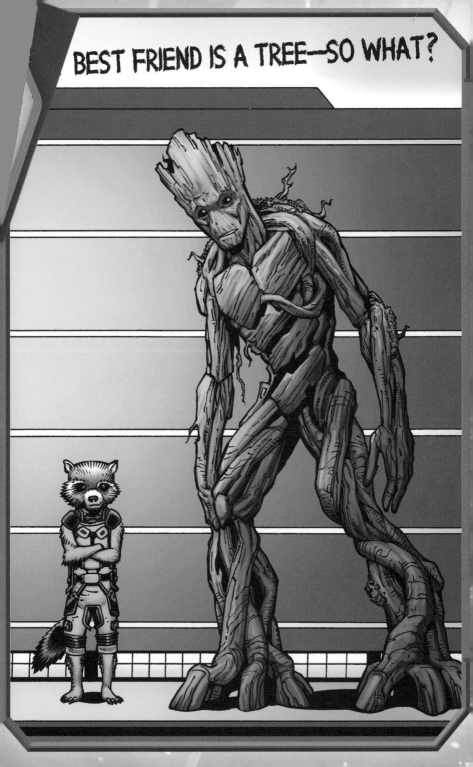

- LET HIM DANCE!

- MAKE SURE HE GETS EIGHT HOURS OF SLEEP EACH NIGHT (UNLESS INTENSE GALAXY SAVING GETS IN THE WAY)

- BAG UP ANY LEAVES HE SHEDS (ESPECIALLY IN THE FALL)

GROOT HEALTH REPORT

ACTUAL SIZE—ISH!

CARE AND KEEPING OF GROOT:

- FEED HIM A BALANCED DIET (YARO ROOT IS OKAY—BUT ONLY IF IT'S RIPE)

- PROVIDE DAILY EXERCISE (TURN OFF THE GRAVITY SO HE CAN SWIM AROUND)

As you may have heard, Groot says only one thing: "I am Groot." Except for once.

We were fighting against this guy, Ronan—a total loser—and were aboard his ship, the <u>Dark Aster</u>. Well, it was going to crash. And Quill and Groot and everyone—including me—were going with it. Destination: Smashed to rubble on the surface of Xandar.

Where was the <u>Milano</u>? Why couldn't we escape? Well, I'd crashed it into the <u>Dark Aster</u> to stop Ronan. Scratch one starship. So we were sitting there, thinking about all the things we wished we'd done in life. Was it sad? You bet.

Suddenly, Groot started growing branches around us, like a shield. He was going to absorb the impact when the <u>Dark Aster</u> crashed. I was pretty sure Groot was going to die. Remember when I said it was sad <u>before</u>? Try now. I was tearing up. Me.

I asked him why he was doing it, and he said, "<u>We</u> are Groot." Can you believe that?

When we crashed, Groot was blown to pieces but—bless that guy—we were all fine. Turns out the fight with Ronan wasn't quite finished but, when it was all over, I picked up a twig off the ground—part of Groot—hoping there was still life left in him. I sure am glad I did.

But giving his life? It's still a mystery to me. So, until I figure it out:

RULE #6

AVOID SELF—SACRIFICE.

Wow, that got pretty sappy. But it helps me make my next point: For every selfless hero like Groot, there are a thousand morons who think they're better than everyone else.

THE UNIVERSE IS FULL OF LOSERS.

Take the Sovereign—if I'd known about them before we took their job, I would have turned off their ship's gravity. I'd love to see them floating around like idiots, because guess what? They think they're perfect.

The Sovereign are genetically programmed, with every possible imperfection removed. I know what you're thinking: Perfect people are good people, right? Wrong.

Instead of perfectly nice, they're perfectly superior scum. They think I'm an abomination, and that Quill is disgusting because he was born outside a test tube. They probably think Gamora is too green, Groot not green enough, and Drax just way too muscular. They might have a point with that last one.

Try working for people who think you're a freak. Do they make you feel valued? Yeah, right! All they care about is their stupid power station and those precious Anulax batteries they don't want busted.

But we had to do the gig—especially considering what they were giving us in return.

I didn't have to like working for them, though. So once that Abilisk hit the ground, I was already thinking of ways to show the Sovereign how imperfect I can be. . . .

By the way, I'm a master of psychology. Not everyone agrees with that, so I'm going to prove it to you.

You'll face lots of folks who think they are, or actually are—temporarily—more powerful than you. They will try to make you feel small and pathetic. You need a way to have your own back.

There is just one problem: Insult them openly and they'll blast you. So what do you do?

RULE #8

TO HIDE AN INSULT, PRETEND IT'S A COMPLIMENT.

I'll explain with an example.

Let's say one of these overblown characters has a reputation for having terrible breath. It's the thing they hate hearing about most in the entire universe. They'd rather have people talk about <u>anything but that</u>.

You say: "I heard your breath is awful, but I'm actually breathing quite well."

See, it sounds kind of like a compliment. If they blasted you, they'd look way too sensitive. But just by bringing up their breath—and let me tell you, it's so thick you might as well be swimming—they get upset. Like you put an Orloni in their underpants, which is actually a good plan B.

So with Ayesha, the Sovereign leader—who's the worst, by the way—I said I'd heard the Sovereign had a reputation for being stuck-up jerks, but then I said they didn't live up to it. I said they were jerks—but without saying so! It still brings a tear to my eye.

Not impressed? Okay, well, <u>that's not all</u> I did.

Life is often about taking things one step further than necessary. Sometimes, the opportunity is too good to pass up. When I get that feeling, I don't think—I act.

Rewind to the power station, right after Gamora turned the Abilisk into a knife throwing demonstration. Now look down. What do you see? That's right, my friends—Anulax batteries. The very same, extremely valuable Anulax batteries we were sent to protect. The same ones those stuck-up Sovereign cared so much about.

You know what I say?

RULE #9

IF YOU CAN'T SHARE IT, YOU DON'T DESERVE IT.

So I stole a few batteries. I know what you're thinking—stealing is wrong. And it can be. But think of it this way: I was educating the Sovereign, showing them the consequences of their snobby attitude. It makes total sense, psychologically. The fact that I benefitted is secondary. Totally.

You might point out that if the Sovereign found out, they'd destroy us. I mean, they almost lasered me just for lipping off to them. But remember: I'm not thinking.

Also, those batteries are worth loads of cash. Get enough of that, you can buy a ship. Get more than enough, you can buy a planet.

Fool that I am, I told Drax about my perfect crime. Why the heck did I brag? I guess I hoped everyone would be too distracted by our official payment for the job. Talk about a hot topic.

Once in a while, you'll have a troublesome passenger. That can be a serious understatement, because guess who the Sovereign handed over to us? Nebula. That's right, Gamora's sister.

Now Nebula is a passenger on the <u>Milano</u>. Normally, we reserve passenger privilege for people who a) are funny, b) like cool music, and c) won't attack us when our backs are turned. While <u>I'm not sure about b</u>, her score is zero everywhere else.

To say Nebula is dangerous is like saying that Yondu can get a little worked up, or that the center of a supernova is a little warm. I guess if you're an adopted daughter of Thanos, danger runs in the family. Go to bed without destroying something, and the day just feels flat.

In situations like this:

RULE #10

THINK SECURITY— YESTERDAY.

Upgrade your holding cell recently? Probably not recently enough—time to install that triple-thick carbon plating. Got beefy shackles? Go back and spring for the Abilisk-grade model. In our case, if there's any Yaro Root lying around, stow it away fast. Nebula's nuts for it.

With Nebula locked up in the back, we took off for Xandar to collect her bounty. At least, that was the plan.

Turns out those Sovereign are perfectly good at math, and realized some batteries were missing. They weren't exactly good sports about it—but neither were my teammates.

POP QUIZ:

Q: What's the hardest thing about being in a team?

A: Your teammates.

Want examples? I've got so many that the sun would burn out before I finished listing them. But really, they all come down to the same two things: Your teammates don't always do what you want, and you don't always do what they want—and then they get upset. Okay, mainly the second thing.

Like here, the Sovereign attacked us. Why? Because I stole those batteries? Sure, maybe, but are we looking deeply into the issue? No! Instead, people just read the headline: ROCKET PUTS FRIENDS IN DIRE JEOPARDY. And then they get angry at me.

For situations like this, I recommend getting defensive and insulting people, because:

RULE #11

IF YOU'RE DEFENSIVE, NOBODY CAN HURT YOU.

Some may say this is a bad rule, but it's always worked for me. And I don't fix what ain't broken.

Because guess what happens when you open up? You get hurt. Like here, it looked like Quill was on my side, like he understood. Turns out he just was being sarcastic, and get this: <u>He hadn't even been using his sarcastic voice</u>. Low blow, Quill.

I was about to retaliate, but the Sovereign were cutting the <u>Milano</u> into bite-size chunks. It was time to get really defensive, and save our skins.

So maybe I landed us in hot water. But compared to what Drax once did, this was a gentle spring shower.

Warning: Worse than not understanding you, sometimes your teammates are a serious danger to themselves—and therefore you. It's that pesky "being a team" thing again.

The time I'm thinking of was when we were on Knowhere, trying to get a meeting with the Collector. Things were a mess. Ever heard the phrase, "morale was in the toilet"? In this case, morale had been flushed all the way to the sewage plant. It hit Drax the hardest.

Some background: I've mentioned Ronan, right? Mean dude, and someone we were on the run from. I considered dyeing my fur just so he didn't know what I looked like. And what does Drax do to the last guy we want to see in the entire universe? He calls him up and tells him exactly where we are.

Why would anyone do such a thing? Well, a little more background, this time on Drax.

Drax is obsessed with Ronan, because Ronan killed Drax's family. Pretty good reason to want revenge, I admit. But here's the problem: it nearly got me killed, along with Groot and everyone else! So:

RULE #12

KEEP AN EYE ON YOUR TEAMMATES AT ALL TIMES.

Not, like, to see if something is going to fall on them so you can warn them to leap out of the way (which is a classy move, by the way). I mean, look out. Because something they do could really mess up your day—or your life.

Lots of people have lost their families. At least they still can feel like they were part of something, once.

But there's nothing like me in the entire galaxy. I'm one of a kind. How's that for making a guy feel lonely?

I'm not "one of a kind" in the way your mom says you are— and not like a snowflake or a fingerprint or some picture your kid sister painted and put on the fridge.

I'm one of a kind like there's nothing even close. Because I was produced. In a lab. By scientists. Not like I asked for it.

Parts of me are, like, alive, and parts of me are mechanical. Cybernetic. To get me this way, I was ripped apart and put back together. Again and again. So remember:

RULE #13

SOMEONE, SOMEWHERE, HAS IT WORSE THAN YOU.

It's not all downside, though. I'm really smart, at least at some stuff. Maybe we could race to see who can dismantle an engine first. I'll win, because I'm really good with machines. Probably comes from being partly made of them.

Being different is a curse, but it can also be a blessing.
Like when a bunch of Sovereign ships are hammering you and
the only escape is through an asteroid field that nobody can
navigate—except you.

At times like that, being different is pretty cool. Just wish
Quill would get the message, too.

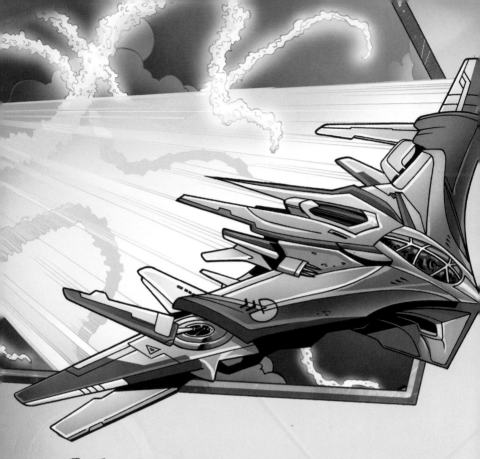

The Sovereign had shown up, shooting holes in the Milano.
You could see space, and not just through the windows. Luckily,
there was a jump point nearby. Great! Except . . .

. . . a quantum asteroid field was in the way.

Imagine a normal asteroid field, but with asteroids a million
times more annoying and deadly. Asteroids might be there, or
they might not. Or more often, they might not be there, and then
suddenly be there—right in front of the ship.

This leads me to a rule that's tough to argue:

RULE #14

LET THE BEST PILOT FLY THE SHIP.

Who's the best pilot in the galaxy? Me, and that's not a brag. It's a fact, like "quantum asteroids can rip you apart," or "the Sovereign are stuck-up nerds." So I flew us in. And because I was flying, we did well. I was dodging asteroids <u>before they even existed</u>.

But then Quill, who can't handle being second best, took over. So I took over again. And then he . . . you get the idea. In the process, we took a hit that knocked out our weapons.

All the Sovereign ships tailing us had crashed into asteroids—except for one that was about to turn us into space dust. And we could only shoot it mean looks. So Drax, sometimes a brilliant, crazy guy, grabbed a rifle and <u>jumped through one of the holes</u> in the back of the ship. Then, Drax shot Mr. Trigger Happy.

Despite Quill being a bit insecure, we made it out of the asteroid field. But it would have been easier if he had just followed my rule.

Before you get the idea that I think Quill's a bad pilot, I'll tell you a story.

Remember when Drax told Ronan we were on Knowhere? Well, Ronan didn't show up alone—he showed up with an army, all flying Necrocrafts. And guess who tagged along? Nebula.

They were pretty serious about getting the Infinity Stone the team was carrying, so Gamora jumped into a mining pod with it and cleared out. Quill and I took two more pods, planning to throw the Necrocrafts off her trail.

The Necrocrafts started firing their Necroblasters—creative namers of things they ain't—and I realized we were in mining pods. In other words, no weaponry.

And then Quill inspired a new rule:

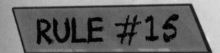

RULE #15

WHEN YOU THINK YOU'RE OUT OF OPTIONS, THINK AGAIN.

He pointed out that our pods were nearly indestructible. We couldn't shoot, but we sure could smash stuff. Have I mentioned that's one of my favorite things?

I flew my pod right at some Necrocrafts—CRASH!—taking out two. Quill knocked the roof off another, flew inside, and used its guns to blast even more Necrocrafts. Slick!

But Nebula chased Gamora into open space, trapping her. Spoiler alert: Gamora wound up fine. In the short term, what looked like a loss was a victory in the end.

Here's an important point: It's the war, not the battle, that matters. <u>Unless I might get killed in the battle</u>—in which case, a little more focus on the battle, all right?

Speaking of facing certain death, remember the quantum asteroid field we escaped? Well, suddenly even more Sovereign ships surrounded us. Some had gone <u>around the field</u>. Who does that? Sooo impolite.

There we were, totally outgunned, our ship full of holes, all weapons offline, Drax dangling out back. And Ayesha—who I'd lipped off to and stole precious batteries from—wouldn't stop until we were turned into debris.

At times like this, I try to adopt a relaxed state of mind. Doesn't sound like me, but it's the truth. If you're a goner, there's no sense getting worked up. The situation's out of your hands, which in a way is good because:

RULE #16   SOMETIMES YOU GET LUCKY.

Out of nowhere, this other ship appeared. To make it extra memorable, a tiny little man was standing on top—and he blew those Sovereign ships away, like a god clearing his nose. As long as he didn't shoot us, we were free to take the jump point.

Entering a jump point is like having your skin stretched out flat while your organs get trampled. With Drax hanging out the back, Gamora had to hold his tether with her hands as we entered hyperspace, so he wasn't left behind. It's not like everything was peachy—but we were alive.

Plus, we were navigating hyperspace, which is one of my specialties.

Space is great—way better than the ground. I don't have to explain that one.

The only problem? Space is really big. Like, unfairly big. Whatever made space really had something to prove. But does that stop us from getting around? No way.

To cross enormous interstellar distances, we use jump points. They're all over the place. By going into one you can pop out another so far away it feels a little like cheating, which is partly why I like them.

You're thinking, "Jump point. Love it. Easy-peasy." Not so fast. Every jump point you pass through does a number on your stomach. So keep trips as short as possible, and for the love of Groot:

RULE #17

NEVER ENTER HYPERSPACE ON A FULL STOMACH.

Leave too much Yaro Root lying around and the crew will feast until it's gone. Then they get sick . . . and I'm not talking about the flu.

Sometimes, you don't have much time to plot a course—possibly when you're chased through an asteroid field. It can be a bit of a dice roll, like how we got to Berhert. I prefer going places that sound interesting, or at least have stuff I want to steal.

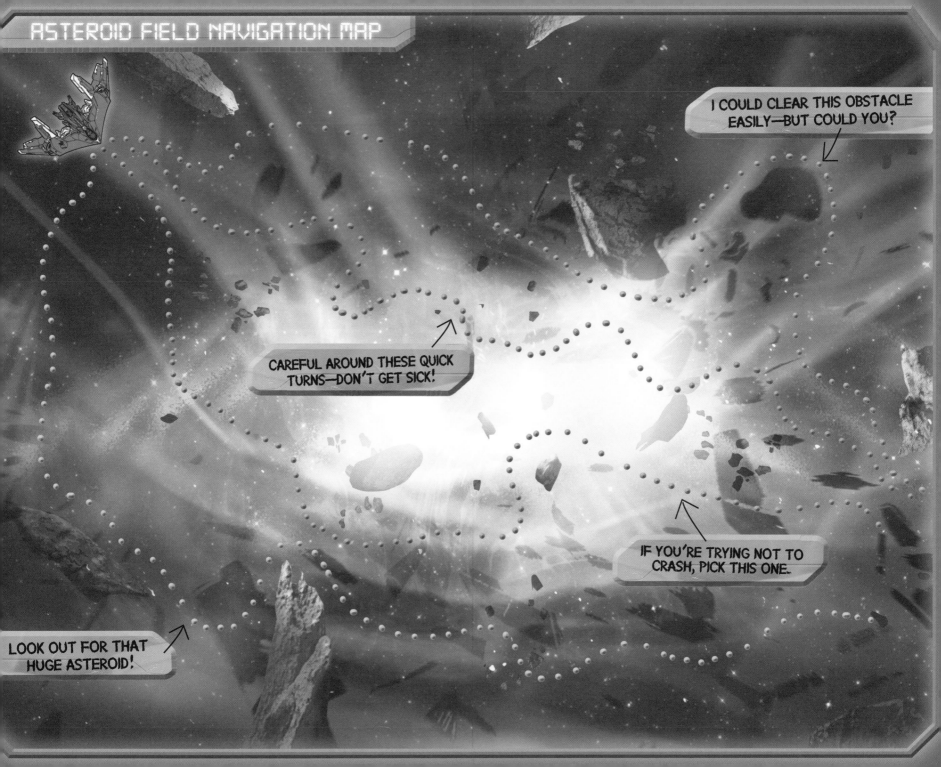

DEFINITELY PRECRASH.

YOU'LL FLY AGAIN, <u>MILANO</u>!

Sure, I like space, but planets are important. They're where y[ou] find neat stuff like air and water, and hopefully someone with a bounty on 'em.

Planets are hard. Not like math—like rock. Unless they're ma[de] of gas or jelly—spent a week on one of those once, very relaxin[g]—they can be pretty determined to stay put. I even have a rule about it:

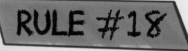

RULE #18

PLANETS DON'T BUDGE.

So flying toward one at enormous speed, uncontrollably, most of your ship's systems offline, isn't exactly a good plan.

If you're ever in the same predicament, I recommend the following:

a) Buckle up. Tricked you! You should be buckled up already.

b) Scream. It'll make you feel better.

c) Is there a larger, softer crewmate nearby? Hug 'em—it might break the impact.

Some say hitting the atmosphere is the worst part. Things are going to get real hot. You're going to notice all the holes in the hull you were supposed to fix, but didn't have time. The worst part is that the atmosphere is very, very soft compared to, say . . .

. . . the surface. Even those soft fluffy trees felt like they were punching the ship. We tore through them, each bump and shake making me think the _Milano_ was going to crack in half.

Eventually, we stopped. We were alive—I knew it. At least until I saw Gamora's face, and thought I might be dead after all.

I respect Gamora. It's automatic for anyone who could kill me in under a second. I'm not a wimp—she's the most dangerous woman in the universe. And that's not just a tough thing to say. Go look it up.

Gamora is also a passionate judge of character—in this case, Quill and me.

Remember when we wouldn't just let the other guy fly the <u>Milano</u> through the quantum asteroid field? To Gamora, this was immature.

THAT'S NOT HER SERIOUS FACE. THAT'S HER FACE.

If you ever face the angry green lady, this next rule might save your life:

RULE #19

WHEN GAMORA'S MAD, KEEP YOUR MOUTH SHUT.

Those thoughts popping into your head to defend yourself? Trust me, they're only going to make it worse.

Then Gamora decided our situation was more my fault than Quill's, just because I stole those batteries. When is that going to be water under the bridge? Quill took this as open season to make fun of me. What's a "trash panda"? I'm pretty sure it's not a nice thing to call someone.

But the most annoying thing is that Drax kept calling them Harbulary batteries. Harbulary? Anulax? Do those sound similar to you? If everyone's going to blame me, at least let's get the words right.

All this, because Gamora decided to teach us a lesson—which nobody asked for.

Luckily, that ship—the one that creamed the Sovereign? It showed up on Berhert.

Before I get to that story, let's make something as clear as "I am Groot": Gamora's record for keeping the team out of danger isn't exactly spotless.

Some background is in order.

Quill likes Gamora, and I can see why. They're about the same height, like to fight, and make witty banter at the same time—it's a match made in heaven. Sure, Drax argues that Quill is a dancer and Gamora isn't—whatever that means in his whack-job world—but I think they're good together. <u>Sometimes too good.</u>

Those sentimental feelings can create big problems for others, like me. Take that battle on Knowhere, when Nebula shot Gamora's pod, leaving Gamora floating in space. Sounds nice and peaceful, right? Actually, she was going to freeze in minutes.

I was ready to give up, but not Quill—he flew out and put his mask on her. He saved her and—in case you ever read this, Gamora—I'm glad he did. But now, <u>Quill was going to freeze.</u> To fix that little problem, h called those Ravager lunkheads—who <u>we were definitely avoiding</u>—who captured them both.

We figured the two soon would be dead, or worse. Here's where I come in, because:

RULE #20

MAKING PEOPLE RESCUE YOU ISN'T HEROIC.

We raced after them and demanded Yondu let them go. Then guess what? Everything was fine. The moment I got involved, everything was quick and easy. Quill would argue that's because he'd already negotiated their release. Personally, I think it's because we brought the Hadron Enforcer.

The Hadron Enforcer is something I thought of, designed, built—the whole shebang. Making stuff like that is kinda my thing, along with being an amazing pilot, escaping prisons, and looking after Groot. I'm what a fancy-pants might call "multifaceted."

Let's get back on topic. Becoming creative with junk you find can save your life. This is especially true in one area: your ship.

If we're passing a salvage yard, I always stop in. But when it comes to salvage, everyone's trying to take your money, so shop smart.

Things to look for:

a) Does it tick? Probably not a good sign.

b) Breaks when you pick it up? Easy—put it back down.

c) Is it shiny? Might be a good find. Just remember:

RULE #21

IF IT'S TOO SHINY, IT'S JUNK.

Eventually you'll find something awesome. You'll be tempted—like me—to walk out without paying. This often is more trouble than it's worth, so get ready to strike a deal.

Carrying Anulax batteries? You can probably trade them for anything. If not, convince the owners that their salvage is trash and <u>they should be paying you</u> to take it away.

Then, get off-world before anyone can think twice, or else they might send their goons after you. But if you make it, boom—the ship can now do something it never could.

Oh, the irony. I'm stuck on Berhert with batteries that are worth their weight in gold, and there's nowhere to trade them. But if there were, oh, the things I would do. . . .

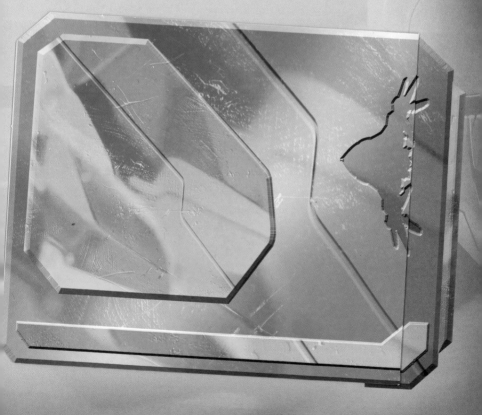

Wondering how I got stuck here all by myself? Well, not totally alone—got Groot to keep me company, and Nebula, though in her case it's more like keeping me on my toes.

Anyway, we were all hanging out on Berhert. Quill talked to the guy from that ship, whose name, turns out, is Ego! Suddenly, Quill says that he and Gamora and Drax are going to leave with the new guy. Seemed like personal business, but aren't we supposed to be a team?

I was upset, but I didn't want to show it. I had to stay back and fix the ship. With what—wood chips? I wanted to make a point, but I didn't want to break one of my most important rules. Some people don't like this one, but it's been with me for a while:

RULE #22

NEVER SHOW YOU CARE.

So, like that thing with the Sovereign, I decided to be indirect about it. Like, be angry, but not make it seem like it was that important.

Basically, I told Quill he was an idiot, which was exactly how I was feeling about him. But I tried to sound cool.

The downside of this approach, I admit, is that people often say something mean in return—which Quill did, asking if I was trying to make everyone hate me. Ridiculous! Still, it stung. Is that actually what I'm doing?

Then, they just packed up and left.

Don't worry. I'll be fine. Let's see what we can find around here to fix this old bird. Who needs a team anyway? Not me! It's not like anything unexpected or dangerous could ever happen on this boring planet!

Wow.

Remember when I said nothing exciting would ever happen on Berhert?

Was I ever wrong.

Before now, I was writing in freedom. Oh, sweet, well-forested Berhert, how I miss you—your trees, your rocks—and the fact that nobody was shooting at me.

Seems I can't help but get caught. That's right, I'm a prisoner again. What makes this a little worse is that this time, it's on a Ravager ship—and it doesn't smell so good.

Of course, I'm getting out. But it's made me think of a new rule:

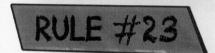

RULE #23

YOU NEVER KNOW HOW GOOD YOU'VE GOT IT.

This goes for lots of things. One minute you're chasing bad guys, the next they're chasing you. Or you've stolen some really cool stuff, and then it gets stolen by someone else. Or—and this one's gonna hurt—one minute you're part of a pretty cool team, and the next they've left you on kinda bad terms.

Maybe I've been a little too hard on the Guardians. But they better be feeling the same way about me! 'Cause if it ain't mutual, I'll be creating a new team—Groot, me, and maybe my newest cellmate. You'll never guess who it is.

Thanos? Not. I'd <u>never team up</u> with that guy.

Nova Prime? She's got pretty interesting hair, but nope.

The Collector? Sure, he's rich, but I'm not a big fan.

Give up? It's Yondu.

Wondering how this happened? Let's go back to Berhert.

How do you repair your ship when you're stranded on a useless planet with no spare parts? Well, in this situation, you've gotta make yourself some spare parts.

Berhert—bless its rocky landscape—wasn't offering much, so it was time to turn to the Milano and see what we had kicking around. She might not be big, but the Milano packs more storage than you'd think.

There were a few lockers I hadn't opened since I joined the team. After all, who knows what Quill's got hidden away? Probably scar me for life.

RULE #24

NEVER LOOK IN QUILL'S LOCKER

Opened everything except that, and my fears were confirmed: We'd been buying stuff for ship defense—not ship repair.

First, I found a bunch of projectile darts, which were a backup system I never installed. Then, some percussive bombs that would make the holes in our ship bigger, not smaller. Finally, some electro discs—pretty good for shocking people, or maybe, in a pinch, rerouting power.

It wasn't a lot, but remember: I'm a genius at this stuff.

Wish I got a chance to prove it, but . . .

. . . the moment I sat down with that junk, I saw something on the scope. Scratch that. <u>Somethings.</u> Lots, closing in through the trees. Unless it was the trees, but I'm pretty sure trees don't walk—unless they're Groot.

Whatever it was, it looked suspicious and I don't take chances—unless I'm betting on Orloni racing, in which case: put everything on the hungriest one. I needed to rig an ambush, fast. And guess what? The stuff I'd found was just what I needed.

Doubting little old me could protect myself? Let's clear that up, rule-style:

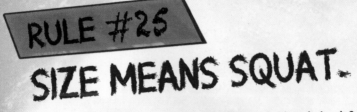

RULE #25

SIZE MEANS SQUAT.

You know what does matter? Strategy. I'm hardwired for that one. Like, if you and I were betting on Orloni I could tell you all my tricks—and I'd still win. You'd be crying so hard, those Orloni would wish they had umbrellas.

The blips were sounding close, so I quickly set my traps. I checked on Groot, and made sure Nebula was still in a foul mood—meaning she hadn't been able to escape. I turned on the stereo, so my possible attackers would think they had nothing to worry about. Then, I spotted them: Ravagers. How the heck did they know where to find us?

I switched everything to hot, just as the first Ravagers crossed the perimeter.

The darts fired, giving a few Ravagers added ventilation. Then the percussive bombs—BRACK! Definitely a repeat purchase. Finally, at close range, I stuck a bunch of them with electro discs. That was like telling twenty-million volts of lightning where to strike. You should have seen the looks on their faces! And they thought I was some little chump.

My traps used up, it turned into a standup fight. I knocked out a few of them pretty good, but then Yondu appeared. This was before we were prison buddies—and more like enemies.

I talk a mean game, even when I'm cornered. But then Yondu started whistling.

As far as I know, Yondu's secret weapon is one of a kind. It's an arrow he controls with his own cybernetics and, get this—whistling! It's really good at flying through things. In this case, the "thing" was going to be my head.

Yondu told me he found the Milano using a tracking device he'd put aboard, way back when we were fighting Ronan on Xandar—and I got mad. I hate sneaky stuff getting on the ship, and almost said something that would've turned me into shish kebab.

Still, as the arrow hovered closer and closer, I realized I had a choice to make.

I'm not a fan of surrender. This should not surprise you. I resist it at all costs. But if I was gone, who would look after Groot? This wasn't gonna happen. I sucked it up and made a new rule:

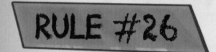

RULE #26

IF IT SAVES YOUR FRIENDS, SURRENDER.

Then, I actually had to admit defeat, out loud, in front of a bunch of people. Ravagers, but still.

Yondu agreed not to hurt Groot, and I was relieved. And then something really weird happened—the Ravagers turned on one another. Before I explain why, I'll cover something I'm familiar with: standoffs.

Remember that time in the Kyln where Quill tried to save Gamora from Drax? She and Drax were at each other's throats. Knives were involved. Things were about to get nasty, but it was like someone pressed pause—this is your classic standoff.

DRAX

GAMORA

RULE #27

CAUGHT IN A STANDOFF? STAND FURTHER AWAY.

If you're nearby, what you really should do is <u>convince them not to fight at all</u>. This can be hard, because the people standing off aren't usually in the mood to listen. But with Drax and Gamora, Quill was real solid—that guy sure knows how to talk. He suggested if Drax really wanted to get to Ronan, he'd be better off letting Gamora stay alive.

Sometimes people don't listen right away, hung up in their anger. I can relate to that. So, for sure, can Drax. But in the end . . . well, you know what happened. Drax and Gamora are both still alive. Even friends, sometimes.

So when I face a standoff of my own, I try to put Quill's methods to use.

I surrendered to Yondu, which was hard enough, but at least I knew what was happening. Then Yondu threw a <u>Milano</u>-size wrench in the works—he decided to let us go.

Good news? Actually, no. To understand why, you need to know something about Ravagers.

RULE #28

A SOFT RAVAGER IS AN EX-RAVAGER

What does that mean? Ravagers are always testing one another—to see who's toughest.

Ravagers are your original tough guys. By their code, there's no room for anyone to be soft. Yondu's the captain, because you could chew him for a week and all you'd do is break off your own jaw. Yondu has to be <u>tougher than everyone in his crew</u>.

Here's the problem: Yondu letting us go, that looked a little too nice. Enough Ravagers thought he was losing his edge that it split the crew right down the middle. That's when the standoff started.

Now, I'm no Quill when it comes to using my vocabulistics to save my skin, but I sure try. If the Ravagers had to fight, I asked, couldn't they at least do it somewhere else?

Suddenly, in the middle of the brawl, Nebula shot the fin right off of Yondu's head. She had gotten free somehow, chomping up all the Yaro Root we had on the ship.

Hey! That was my dinner!

I thought they were going to lock Yondu and me up right away, but they didn't. Instead of a simple prison break, we were strapped down in front of the new Ravager captain.

This jerk took all the Ravagers who had refused to mutiny and flushed them out the airlock. Then he turned to us. I got worried it might turn into an interrogation.

You can't let an interrogation succeed, because that means you've probably told the interrogator something important. This always leads to something bad.

On the other hand, these Ravagers had Groot, so if we resisted he might get hurt. I had to play it smart. Remember how I'm a master of psychology?

RULE #29

DON'T ANSWER QUESTIONS, ASK THEM.

The new Ravager boss told us his name was Taserface—his first mistake. When you pick a name, don't pick one so easy to make fun of. He told me it was a metaphor. I asked him to explain the metaphor. Then he really got mad.

Little-known fact about Taserface: When he gets upset, he starts close talking. We're talking saliva like a monsoon. I thought I was going to need a boat. I made my disgust clear, and Taserface threatened to shut me up, once and for all. It was looking like airlock time with no spacesuit for yours truly .

Right then, Nebula piped up, insisting we be kept alive. Only so she could turn us over to our enemies but still, Nebula really saved us there. Unpredictable girl.

I couldn't resist making fun of Taserface. People are always calling me names. If I had a mom, she'd probably say it's because they're jealous. I think it's because I'm different. Different wigs people out.

In space, folks look all kinds of strange. Take Groot, or Drax, even Quill—who's to say he's normal? Point is, you probably look weird to somebody. Get ready for a few insensitive remarks.

RULE #30

MAKE THEM PAY.

For a long time I went all out when someone called me a name. I'd put knock-out gas in someone's air tanks, or reprogram his or her navigation computer to fly straight into a planet made of sewage.

Since then, I've matured. Which—for me—means an eye for an eye. Someone calls me something, I call them something. Takes less effort.

Have to admit, I feel like I still haven't solved this one, especially with the Guardians. Quill's always calling me names, and I'm always insulting him in return. It's hard to tell who started it, and who's just keeping it going.

Maybe payback's not actually all it's cracked up to be, at least sometimes. Want an example of what I mean? Turn the page.

HERE ARE SOME NAMES **NOT** TO CALL ME!

RULE #31

SOMETIMES PAYBACK'S NOT WORTH IT.

I never liked Nebula, not since the first moment she tried to kill me. Maybe I'm a little sensitive, or maybe I just like to keep living. Anyway, she's near the top of my list of people to stay several light years away from.

She's still deadly, still so moody it makes me want to bang my head against the Milano. But recently, I'm seeing her differently.

I used to think Thanos—who's so bad he makes Ronan look like a baby—was Nebula's father. Turns out, that's not exactly true. Thanos adopted Nebula and Gamora after he killed their families. Legal? Not in this sector.

Then, Thanos really did a number on Nebula. He made her fight against Gamora, who always won. He experimented on her and "upgraded" her, to see if she would win the next time. Not so different from what happened to me. So, I can understand why she's angry.

The danger of anger, though, is that it can make you do things you later regret—if you're still alive to have regrets afterward, that is. What Nebula's planning to do, I'm not so sure she will be.

Nebula's taken off to fight Gamora, desperate to beat her just once. What will that solve? Nothing. Plus, Gamora is going to annihilate her. Nebula might never walk again, and that's if she's lucky.

I'D RATHER BE AN ORPHAN THAN HAVE THANOS AS A DAD!

So, here I am in prison. Still. With Yondu, and guess what he's doing? Moping. Can you believe it? It's the last thing I expected from the guy, which proves that:

RULE # 32

ANYONE CAN SURPRISE YOU.

Ever since the Ravagers who took over flushed the Ravagers loyal to Yondu out the airlock, he's been miserable. I can't get him to laugh at anything—not even my Taserface impression. Maybe I'm spitting too much.

I really believed Yondu was as mean as he seemed, but some acts are so good you can't tell. It's a hard galaxy, and it makes people hard, too. Pretty soon, they're hiding stuff inside that's actually pretty good.

Heck, maybe I do that, too. Sure would explain why people think I'm being mean when I'm actually trying to be nice.

Maybe they should try to understand harder!

Personally, I prefer the new Yondu. He really cared about his crew. Makes me think about Quill, Drax, and Gamora. Do I . . . miss them? Maybe I do. I sure hope they're okay. If not, maybe they need help—and I'm stuck in this prison!

Time to get Groot away from Taserface and bust out of this joint!

Yondu says he has a way to escape. I'm turning over a new leaf—I'm gonna let his plan play out. For starters, it saves me a ton of work. Plus, <u>we're on his ship</u>—he might have an edge.

Before you get any ideas, though, that doesn't make him the ranking expert. <u>That's me.</u>

If you're unconvinced, I have proof I'm a master jailbreak artist—the high points of how I got everyone out of the Kyln. There are some advanced ideas here, so pay attention.

RULE #33

IF THERE'S A WAY IN, THERE'S A WAY OUT.

Some say the Kyln is the hardest place in the whole galaxy to break out of. I'd put it at Number Four. I've broken out of at least three prisons that were harder. Prison Number One? <u>You don't even know you're in prison.</u> Try breaking out of that one, kids.

The moment we showed up at the Kyln, I could see they'd gone for a selective gravity system. They thought it would be secure, but it was actually a weakness.

That's what gave me the idea to switch off gravity everywhere but the guard tower, and fly that back to the <u>Milano</u>. Which is exactly what we did.

I'm not expecting this level of genius from Yondu. In fact, the thought of teaming up with him is still weirding me out a little.

Of all the things I imagined happening in my life, breaking out of a cell with Yondu was definitely <u>not one of them</u>. A heated argument with Yondu? Sure. Laying a trap that would dunk Yondu in slime? I was hoping. Definitely not this, but it helps make a point:

RULE #34

SOMETIMES YOUR TEAMMATES AREN'T WHO YOU EXPECT.

You gotta put aside your differences with others, at times, because there's a bigger goal—like getting the heck away from Taserface. It's the heroic thing to do. Plus, it might be your only way out. Let me explain.

We were defending Xandar from Ronan. We had to keep him from reaching the planet surface, and we were getting our butts kicked. Right when I thought we didn't have a chance, guess who showed up? The Nova Corps!

Until then, the Nova Corps were on top of my list to fire out an airlock into a black hole, especially Denarian Saal—I'd have sent him out the airlock without his pants. But there he was, offering his assistance.

It was strange, being side by side with Saal, protecting those nincompoops the Xandarians, feeling friendship from the Nova Corps. And you know what? We made a pretty good team. But then . . . they all got blown away.

I got real, real mad. There's one thing you don't do to Rocket: Take out his friends, even new ones. So I rammed the <u>Milano</u> into the <u>Dark Aster</u>, saving Quill and the others. Because of that, we later stopped Ronan.

If the Nova Corps hadn't helped, I probably wouldn't be here. I know, embarrassing but true. I'm hoping Yondu comes through like they did—and survives.

I'm so angry I might punch holes through this paper. Groot just showed up outside the cell, shaking like a leaf—all right, more like a branch—dressed like a Ravager! Taserface has been messing with him. Makes me wish I had a Hadron Enforcer right now!

So, a little entry on all the creeps—the Ronans, the Thanoses, the freaking Taserfaces. What Taserface pulled reminds me of another grade A dork—the Collector.

RULE #35

KNOW YOUR ENEMIES.

Back on Knowhere, we finally got a meeting with the Collector—I guess he owns the whole place. Strange thing to own, a giant floating head. Probably should have realized right there that the guy was off.

We walked into an area stacked with cases and cages full of creatures—trapped!—from all over the universe. This guy was really bad news. Then, when he saw Groot, the Collector was ready to cut a deal for him. To that fool, Groot was just an object with no feelings, something to acquire. Guess what I said? Well, that almost blew the whole deal. All that matters is that Groot and I made it out.

Stay on guard for jerks who want power over others. They're the worst. Not that anyone could actually control Groot. Like, get ready for a few laughs at what Yondu's trying to get him to do!

OPEN HERE

Yondu's escape plan ain't starting strong.

See, Groot's not known for being a big thinker. He's a tree of many strengths—but he probably won't cure diseases, solve impossible math formulas, or find a way to make Quill shut up for five minutes. And <u>Yondu's plan depends on Groot</u> finding something for us.

RULE #36

DON'T RELY ON GROOT'S ABILITY TO REMEMBER.

I told you about Yondu's arrow. He flies it by whistling, but without that fin on his head, the arrow goes nowhere. And . . . Nebula blasted the fin off.

Another fin is kept in the captain's quarters (where Taserface is probably dreaming up mean things to do to us).

Yondu sent Groot there to bring it back. Simple enough. Except Groot's been there for hours.

<u>He was supposed to get a fin.</u> You know, you might recognize it for a fin, because it's fin-shaped. But guess what he brought back, instead?

- Yondu's underpants (Nasty!)

- An Orloni (Tell me, does a fin have four legs and bite?)

- Vorker's cybernetic eye (Reminds me of something I want to tell you.)

- A desk (I'd like to see that on Yondu's head.)

- A toe (Even nastier!)

We better figure this out, and quick, even though I'd stick around just to see Vorker without his eye.

Everyone knows I like to steal stuff. But there's a special kind of stuff I like stealing most: prosthetics. If there's a guy with a fake leg or plastic arm, I try to get it from him.

Why? Mainly for the money—prosthetics can get pretty expensive. Round up a few legs and exchange them for an upgraded shield generator. A few arms could equal beefier plumbing—something we've needed, thanks to Drax.

But I have to admit, there's another reason: It's funny! A one-legged guy hopping around makes me laugh so hard my tail might fall off. And a guy with no nose has a face so flat you could use it as a bookend.

STEALING PROSTHETICS IS FUN AND PROFITABLE.

Okay, mostly fun, I admit.

I don't know why it cracks me up so much. Maybe those poor folks with prosthetics and I have something in common—we've all been cut up and mixed with machinery. So, you could say I'm doing it because of something that happened to me, because it's actually not funny.

I never thought of that before now. I guess sometimes we laugh at what hurts us. Whatever. Maybe it's true, maybe not—I'm just gonna think about how much it makes me laugh.

Anyway, I've got another distraction. Someone brought us Yondu's new fin. It wasn't Groot—but Kraglin!

KRAGLIN

TASERFACE

Thanks to Kraglin, we've got everything we need to bust out of this greasy cell.

Maybe you don't know him. Kraglin's Yondu's first mate, or he was before the mutiny. Yondu and Kraglin have known each other forever. But when Taserface went against Yondu, Kraglin went, too. You know how blue Yondu is? By joining the other side, Kraglin made Yondu so mad he turned purple.

I'm not surprised Kraglin was fed up working for Yondu. I bet that's part of the reason Quill split—that, and the constant threat of getting eaten.

Then Kraglin had a new problem: working for Taserface. Sure, Yondu can be a pain, but <u>Taserface</u>? I'd almost rather work for Ronan. Almost.

But remember, everyone who stayed loyal to Yondu got thrown out the airlock. Within ten seconds, they were as cold and hard as meat from the back of your freezer. So Kraglin's thinking, Do I want to end up like an ice block?

Even if Kraglin's not exactly a genius, he's not dim-witted enough to feel "career satisfaction" working for a guy who thinks "taser" and "face" sound cool together. Puts Kraglin in a difficult position: Change sides? Luckily for us, Kraglin took the plunge. When we strap the new fin on Yondu, he can fly his arrow.

So here's the lesson. If you end up fighting on the wrong team, keep in mind:

RULE #38

IT'S NEVER TOO LATE TO CHANGE SIDES.

Before I forget, there's someone else I'd love to drop this wisdom on.

If there's one person who needs to reevaluate things, it's Nebula. She's probably close to confronting Gamora now, itching for victory. Either that or she's already in pieces so small you'd mistake her for dandruff.

I'm fairly certain what Nebula wants isn't to make war, <u>it's to make peace</u>. Can she realize it, too? She'd have to overcome her bitterness, all those years of feeling like her life didn't mean anything until she won. She has to realize that more than an enemy, what she really wants is a sister.

It's going to be rough. When we have a <u>reason to be angry</u>, we probably have a reason to stay angry. If it goes for me, sure as Groot hates hats, it goes for Nebula, too.

I hope Nebula figures this out. Trust me—as someone who has seen Gamora fillet an Abilisk, she makes a way better ally than opponent.

RULE #39

SOMETIMES YOUR OLD ENEMY IS YOUR NEW BEST FRIEND.

Does anyone you're fighting with fit this picture? Try to put your differences behind you. All that energy you're using against each other could be used for doing something awesome, instead.

We're about to attempt our escape—this might be my last entry. So, a final shout-out to the Guardians! They taught me there's <u>nothing better than being on the right team</u>.

After Knowhere, Ronan was in possession of the Infinity Stone and was going to use it to destroy Xandar. This situation brought the Guardians to a turning point.

We had a taste of how well we worked together. It was exciting, but some of us—Quill—were <u>a little too excited</u>. Quill started talking about <u>going after Ronan</u>—Ronan, who is ordinarily scary, but now had an unstoppable weapon. If Quill's plan was mind-blowing, maybe I was in, but . . .

Quill had only 12% of a plan. If a whole plan is the <u>Milano</u>, then 12% is the light that tells you when someone's using the bathroom, more or less. I laughed at him—because <u>that wasn't a plan</u>.

So for the Guardians to stay together, we had to use a 12% plan to stop 100% of the end of the world.

What happened next proves that when you find the right team, anything is possible. The others started standing up, joining Quill—including Groot. Soon, I was alone. Then I realized that trying to do something important even if you fail is better than doing something meaningless even if you succeed.

So I stood up, too.

RULE #40

MEANINGFUL FAILURE BEATS EMPTY SUCCESS.

I felt like an idiot but, in the end, this insane mission is one of the proudest moments of my life. Your friends can make you do the impossible. It's part of why you need them.

ESCAPE!

I wasn't sure Yondu would pull it off, but turns out he had a little secret to reveal for the perfect moment—Rocket style.

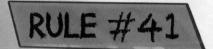

RULE #41

ALWAYS KEEP A TRICK UP YOUR SLEEVE.

Let's back up.

I strapped the new fin to Yondu's head. It was a big, fancy prototype and made him impressively tall. Then Yondu whistled for the arrow—awesome!—but this alerted the Ravagers. <u>All of them</u>. Loading their guns, they closed in on the cell, ready to take us out. Meanwhile, I was empty-handed. Yeah, awkward.

The Ravagers attacked. Yondu's arrow whistled everywhere, dropping guys left and right, but the Ravagers kept coming. Groot even tackled one—that's how desperate we were. Sure, we played some music for fun, but it was <u>serious</u> fun.

And then, Yondu did something that looked really bad.

As you're aware, I know engines. If there's one thing I'm certain about, it's that <u>you don't puncture them</u>. But that's exactly what Yondu did—he flew his arrow right through the engine. Like I expected, the engine started to explode, <u>taking the ship down with it</u>. I figured Yondu had done us in. But instead of breaking a blue sweat, he told Kraglin to release the <u>Quadrant</u>—and I realized that blowing up the engine was part of his plan.

The <u>Quadrant</u>, I discovered, is a mini-ship hidden within the larger one. Soon, the only thing Taserface was ravaging was asteroid dust. Meanwhile, we zipped off safe and sound in some pretty comfy seats.

Slick work, Yondu.

After escaping on the <u>Quadrant</u>, we needed to find the other Guardians fast—meaning hyperspace. If that meant taking us through <u>more jump points than anyone has ever done</u>, so what?

Yondu was yelling to stop. Guess he was tired from all that escaping. Sorry, bro!

We passed through hundreds of jump points, blipping past planet after planet. Out the window, flashes went by so fast my head was going to explode—not to mention my stomach. On some planets, strange monsters were duking it out. Others were pink and covered in funky amoebas. Some weren't planets at all—just asteroids where Watchers, I dunno, watched. All these crazy, unique places—I realized they were like you and me. One of a kind.

Sure, diversity is what makes the universe so complicated and frustrating. Walking different, talking different, feeling different—sometimes it's not pretty. But diversity is also what makes the universe interesting. I'd much rather be a weirdo than the same as everyone else.

Whenever you're down because you're feeling like an outsider, remember this:

RULE #42

FEELING DIFFERENT? DEAL WITH IT.

Because when it's really important, diversity is key to staying alive. I've got a story to prove it. Spoiler alert: It's from the time we saved the galaxy.

After the Dark Aster crashed on Xandar, we thought Ronan was beat. He wasn't.

Ronan had stashed the Infinity Stone inside his hammer. If that touched the ground—which is a big, easy target—it would destroy all life on the planet.

Quill kept him distracted with a funky dance, while I fixed the Hadron Enforcer as fast as I could. We'd already shot Ronan with it once with less than stellar results, so where did we aim this time? His hammer.

BOOM.

The hammer exploded, releasing the Infinity Stone, which started falling toward the ground. Inches from lights out on Xandar, and what did Quill do? He caught it.

The Stone's energy will rip anyone apart, and Quill started to vaporize. He looked done, but Gamora reached for his hand—absorbing some of the power. Now they both were going to fry. So Drax did the same thing. I thought, What the heck?—and joined the circle of pain.

We were all holding hands. Friendly, except a power older than the universe was peeling the skin off our bodies. We should have died. Instead, we stopped Ronan.

RULE #43 DIVERSITY CAN SAVE THE DAY.

Now I know part of why we survived is that Quill is special. But the stone looked like it was beating him. He needed our help. I wonder if we oddballs hadn't come together with our unique weirdnesses, would Xandar exist today?

I don't think so.

We've almost reached the Guardians. Yondu must have guessed that I miss them, because he stepped into Gamora's place and took me to school.

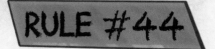

RULE #44

BE READY TO LEARN ABOUT YOURSELF.

I don't recommend taking advice. Most of the time I blow it off. This time, my gut reaction was to see if the <u>Quadrant</u> had an ejector seat—<u>for Yondu or me</u>. It doesn't, but I knew I should listen anyway, to see if what he said made sense.

And it did.

Remember those batteries? The ones I stole that got us into trouble in the first place? I'm not sure why I took them. Sure, it was fun, and also made a point—but deep down, <u>why did I do it</u>? Enter Yondu.

Yondu said that like him, I've got a hole inside of me—cut out by every bad thing that's ever happened, by those scientists who experimented on me, by stuff I don't even remember. He said I stole those batteries to try and fill that hole. He's right. I mean, I told him to take a hike—but he's right. It's got me thinking.

Sometimes, when I'm not thinking, <u>it seems like I'm making the choices</u>—but maybe I'm not. Maybe it's that hole shouting at me to fill it, and I'm obeying because I don't notice. Well, listen here! I'm going to start paying attention.

I sure hope Quill and the gang haven't gotten blasted, because:

NOBODY CAN DO IT ALONE.

I might be one tough cookie, but if I want to do something really big, I need backup. Everybody does.

I fought this idea at first. People are unpredictable, crazy, smelly in ways I can't explain, and often do things that could have me blown up. By now, though, I've seen enough to know that working with others is worth putting up with, because we can do way more together than we can do by ourselves.

The hardest part is realizing it goes two ways: They need me and I need them. This is tough for a guy who on some days would rather be on an asteroid orbiting a moon hidden inside a black hole. But I got used to Groot—what's a few more weirdos in the mix?

After what I said to Quill, not to mention stealing those batteries at maybe the worst possible time, I'm not sure the Guardians will want to see me. But I hope so.

WITH FRIENDS LIKE THESE, I DON'T MIND LOOKING SHORT.

We just pulled into orbit. Guardian reunion, here I come! Time to save a bit of the galaxy.

Feeling fired up, hero-style? Hope so, because <u>we need you</u>. We can be in only one place at a time, and remember how annoyingly big the universe is? Plus, there seems to be no end to creeps like Ronan, Thanos, and the Sovereign.

Going up against those jerks isn't the only way to save the galaxy. Take a look around—there might be a way to save a corner that's staring you in the face. While you're figuring out what to do, I'll give my best shot to be a better teammate. But let's not get too carried away.

Until you hear from me again, remember:

RULE #47

KEEP YOUR EXPECTATIONS REALISTIC.

Oh, and if the Nova Corps pulls you over while you're reading this book—I suggest eating it.

Writer: Matt Sinclair
Editor: Amy Nathanson Heaslip
Art Director and Designer: Andrew Barthelmes
Copy Editor: Mary Bronzini-Klein
Managing Editor: Christine Guido
Creative Director: Julia Sabbagh
Associate Publisher: Rosanne McManus
Marvel Team: Sarah Brunstad, Nick Fratto, David Gabriel,
    Jeffrey Reingold, Daniel Schoenfeld
Disney Team: Chelsea Alon, Kurt Hartman, Colin Hosten,
    Tomas Palacios, Eugene Paraszczuk

Studio Fun International
An imprint of Printers Row Publishing Group
A division of Readerlink Distribution Services, LLC
10350 Barnes Canyon Road, Suite 100
San Diego, CA 92121
www.studiofun.com

Studio Fun International is a registered trademark of Readerlink
Distribution Services, LLC.
All notations of errors or omissions should be addressed to
Studio Fun International, Editorial Department, at the above
address.
ISBN: 978-0-7944-4070-1
Manufactured, printed, and assembled in China.
21 20 19 18 17 1 2 3 4 5

Conforms to ASTM F963